THE SUN WATCHES THE SUN

THE SUN WATCHES THE SUN

DEJAN STOJANOVIĆ

Translated by the Author

New Avenue Books

THE SUN WATCHES THE SUN
English translation Copyright © 2012 Dejan Stojanović

The Sun Watches the Sun is the English translation of the poetry collection *Sunce sebe gleda*, originally written in Serbian and published in 1999 in Belgrade by *Književna reč*.

New Avenue Books

First Edition in English

Library of Congress Control Number: 2024951430

ISBN-13: 979-8-9919466-9-8

Contents

SKY-MOTION

A light cloud
Moves into the night
Igniting the world and
Turning movement
Into sky-motion

THE MOST BEAUTIFUL POEM

I wanted to write the most beautiful poem
But that is impossible,
The world has written its own.

FIRST SILENCE

Hurrying to learn the secret signs
Hunted by your own dreams
Of the first picture on the final night
Seduced, you levitate over
A vast, bottomless Universe

Praying for the strength you go farther
Move to foreign lands to find their dreams
To check if you'll know
What kind of secret lies within you

Seeking to sense the essence of all
Over which the first silence sleeps
Amazed by the heavenly mirage
Your dream tries to find itself

TOP AND BOTTOM

By playing with sound and shape
You make an appearance on this side;
Arching the sky, you hide its Source
The very habitat of truth.

Over the stormy sea of a dream
You quiet the unbridled bottom of your own
In primordial chaos' storms
Reconciling states of Space and Chronos

With a secret seductive scent,
The veil of endless high seas
Says you are the sole purpose, the Supreme Entity,
Falling from your own top to your own bottom.

MARKED BY INFINITY

Marked by the sea, marked by infinity
I last this one day and disappear.
With the sea, I merge
Again, with infinity in the pre-being.

Between crucified oblivions
By a marked silence enslaved
Immeasurable bliss I find—
The mountain top of the sky.

WINDMILL

Seductive embers—soft gleams
Borne by the game—covering coldness
Enchanting chants—reflex of bliss
In the land of spirit—somewhere far

Storm in the head—mover of spirit
Echoes' formidable force
While loneliness alone
Hovers over its emptiness

HOLY FIRE

Holy fire glistens from the Source
Of the world and fire

From whirlwinds into nebulas
Fire spreads into the heights
Enabling microns with full force

Lonely bodies in emptiness hang,
Followers full of force
Are their only accompaniment

VORTEX

The first night lasted long,
Dreamed long,
Before it shone.

The night was everything;
Everything was the night.

How the dot shone
And broke the harmony of the night
Nobody will understand
Ever.

COSMOS

Cosmos is the body
That brought forth the secret

Cosmos is God
Who whispered the syllable of life

COSMOS' FLOWER

From his hand
A flower has arisen
Spreading out the scent of the Source
Revealing the way to the first beat

A festive flower dances
Whipping-top that doesn't choose the place
But with every jump, it is wider
By unrest, it pledges peace

ARE YOU, OR ARE YOU NOT

Are you the world or an apparition
Are you the truth or simply flight

Do you sleep or only dream
Do you exist or practice sorcery

Are you, or are you not

GOD AND CIRCLE

THE DAY OF THE UNIVERSE

All is a Circle
With motion, we pay back the debt
Everything wants the old peace
Through storm to touch the Circle

Through shape into an unshaped
Secret, through omnipotent
Moment of this day's dream
To the Heart of the Universe

SKY AND CIRCLE

By circling into a circle
Behind the circle-by-circle
Moving in a circle of a circle

By quark into a quasar
Only one image, by a circle
Into a shape was transformed

Circle the circle circles
The sky serves as a canvas
A pledge to permanent friendship

Between a Circle and a Circle
Of an Ultimate Circle
In the Heart of the Being

TRUTH OF THE CIRCLE

You look high up, then
Down. You don't see much
But a bond is there—
Widening the heights
Thickening the ground.

The Truth of the Circle
Engulfs infinity;
In it dispersed
Over it clear
Essence resides.

GOD AND CIRCLE

The Circle is our origin
Never leaving,
We open the door to enter another circle.

Where is the door that leads outside,
Is there an exit?
Or, is God a Circle
In which we live fed by Him

SKYWALKING

RAIN OF THE ABSOLUTE

You are here, and you are not
Unaware it is you what we see
We fly forward with your wings
Yet we do not recognize you

It has been a long time since you glowed
Nevertheless young
Your dream is the dream of those
Who will dream of you

Life is only a flicker of melted ice
Stars are only the rain of the Absolute

A CLOUD

God is the cloud
From which rain fell

Rain moistened the emptiness
Inseminated emptiness gave birth to the Universe
The rest is motion

The cloud transformed into yet another
Attempting to remember its form
And return to the cosmic Embryo

CLOUD II

Cloud and its image surround you.
Through a cloud, you move into the world
And from the world—through a cloud, as well.

What kind of a dream is one
In which you dream with open eyes?

Used to miracles,
Tired, you watch hurried tenants of the Cosmos

Yet, this game rejoices you
That was not easy

LIGHT AND NIGHT

Light is a trait
Darkness is only a word that names darkness
But darkness you need not describe
Unconceived
From time immemorial—
Always, forever, everywhere
Light is dawning
Sublime
Darkness is infinitely deep
It is impossible to penetrate its depths
Darkness is quite
While light speaks
Light is newer, fresher
Darkness was here before the light
Still, darkness is younger
Darkness does not age
Nothing is always nothing

A DECEIT

In the essence of truth lies deceit
Without it, the truth would be meaningless
There would be ice only.
The first essence uses magic to save itself
Nature's laws are part of this magic.
Truth gave itself shape and order.
Divided, we acquire new truths.
A child longs to return to eternal Mother
Diversity rushes to unite
Deceit dispels the boredom of the Absolute
It's a game with only one player
In which he forgets himself
So that he would have something
To fulfill motion while returning.
Absolute equals nothingness
Immobile and mute.
Omnipotence and omniscience
Are the end of power and knowledge.
The secret is imperfection,
Desire to reach the zenith.
Deceit doesn't lessen us but itself
That is why we cannot accuse it of deceit

THE YOUNG OLD BEING

Everything and nothing
Are the same in the Absolute

Condemned to immobility
It has to divide

Saved by division
It discovers itself and hurries back

The more divided
The better

Nourished by shapes
Sphere is its life

This way, the old being
Stays always young

ETERNITY AND EXISTENCE

Procreation annihilates eternity
In existence, there is a birth
Existence is the end of endless eternity
Without the beginning and end

Unborn eternity doesn't die.
Existence is dying
To fall asleep in eternity
Beyond Existence

ETERNITY AND ETERNITY

Eternity is a glorious word
But eternity is ice

Knighthood lies above eternity
It doesn't live off fame but rather deeds

Our eternity is not real
It resembles us—it is our invention
Its scent is vanity

ZERO

God walks through wide spaces;
Our thoughts, too

It's easy to divide spaces into other spaces
In thoughts

We divide them and divide
And divide even more

Dividing them, we still walk
Through wide spaces

The narrow region we cannot divide,
We never find

More and more, we divide space
In wide spaces

Thus, following God
Zero, we never find

SPEED

Love of a body toward another body
Is the Source of speed

Speed keeps the balance
Keeps the family together

Speed makes bodies stable
Defends them from chaos

INFINITY AND END

Infinity is the end
Story ends here

End without infinity
Is but a new beginning

Invisible flow
Creates the balance of reality

Force from within and external force
Warm us

The world is God's salvation

FORGOTTEN PLACE

HEARTHSTONE

Sun is a Hearthstone
A merry-go-round of extinguished hearthstones

On such hearthstones
Those who see the light are born

That is how the Hearthstone sees itself
Inspires and continues

The Universe is the Sun watching itself

A FAIRY TALE AND THE END

The world is a fairy tale
We are its guardians

Attached to the ground
We daydream of the end

We long for eternity
Between the two ends

Two forces create eternity
A fairy tale and a dream
From the fairy tale

A PARADOX

Dwarf: Tell me the truth
I can take it

Secret: If you could take it
I might tell you

Dwarf: That is a paradox
Secret: Truth is a paradox

GOD'S APPRENTICE

You are not God
You are everywhere and nowhere

Who are you
What are you looking for?
You always appear at the wrong time

You always flout
Yourself and others
You cry over the holy mirage

Are you the chimera
Afraid of other chimeras
You wander far from yourself to yourself

Has anyone ever seen you
Or do we only dream of you

BUBBLE

You appeared here alone
Without asking anybody
Nor has anybody asked you

You are here now
But you cannot change anything
You walk

Moving through the dream
To a new delay, a malaise
To the new beam or the new deceit

You wait and watch there
From where you came
In this deceitful corner of the Universe

SOLID GROUND

By anathema or by blessing
You are limited to that form
To walk through the world

To cheer and fall
Trying to reach
That for which you bode
That which won't be accessible

You look at the heights, always aware
Between these heights
And the life of other species
You stand with eyes turned to the sky

GOD IS BUSY

Only a few things interest you
Others are interested in everything

From a few things, everything else comes
You defend yourself

There is no difference between big and small
They are all variations

Others are sunbathing
You think of God

And when you are most furious with him
You crave him the most

But God is busy
And has no time for you

STAR IN THE GRASS

Get close to the grass
And you'll see a star

Accept the smiling light
Of another soul if it comes your way

All light of the world is in you
Sunbath from within

Dissolve the rest with glances
Their reverse is different

Go back to your old habit
Of looking at the sky

Collect from its fields
And you will become sweet-smelling

That's how another enlightened soul
Can smell a newly invented scent

And join you in finding the first star
In the cluster of stars spreading at your feet

HIS LETTER

Toward an invisible face
Toward its letters
Letter by letter toward the center

Getting closer
To earn redemption

Predicting foggy contours
With which emptiness draped itself
To protect us from coldness and ice

FORGOTTEN PLACE

We think the dream place doesn't exist
And that is only the forgotten place awakening in us

That place is not a fairy tale
Rather unreachable truth
To remind us we were something else

The place we dream of wakes us up
In the middle of light
That resembles a fairy tale

FIRE

Where is fire
To melt the icy Circle?

Where is the answer
For even a little sign?

A beam of light moving through this fairy tale
While we try to find the best way

RETURN

Arrival in the world
Is really a departure

And that, which we call departure,
Is only a return

A STONE AND A WORD

WHERE DOES A SONG END

How many languages are there in the Universe?
Can we ever hear them, not to mention learn them?
Even earthly languages are often beyond our reach.

How many books were written,
Paintings and histories that are different from ours?
We don't know anything about that.

Who are their Caesars and Napoleons?
Their Homers and Shakespeares, their prophets
And where are they now?

About all this, we know nothing.
Even about ourselves
We don't know much more.

A WORD

Grows into a meaning
And flies from it

Causes Happiness or
Makes us unhappy

The same words we love and hate
Leave in different directions
Taking different paths

A FIRST WORD

The moment when the first word was born,
When a mute first spoke,
How long did that moment last?
What was it like?

How many seconds or years
Were needed for a second or a third word,
How long for a language
And then to divide languages and people?

What was necessary
To forget that we are indeed the same

A STONE AND A WORD

Awakening of the world is the speech of a stone
It has its story and its secret

A stone is an eye and an ear
It watched the light, listened to the water
Moved everywhere
Came from darkness

Although it willingly forgets
Its memory is the longest

Without oblivion, stone's word has no meaning
Words are its desire to remember

That futile job
Stone diligently performs

Life of a stone is a life of self-examination
Listening to oneself

COMBINING WORDS

In the chaos
Words sleep and wait
Their life depends on our choices

From the moment we assemble words,
They are alive
They are not only words now but meanings

They caress and scratch
Invisibly enter our being,
Building their hideouts
Thunder from unexpected places

HIDDEN WORDS

While we look for them
They hide
Deeper and deeper
As though connected by force, they fight

Through words
To the meaning of thoughts
With no words

Different languages
Same thoughts
Servants to thoughts
And their masters

UNUTTERED WORDS

How many unuttered words
Died in the heads
Of those for whom a word
Was too expensive

STORIES

Everybody talks,
But there is no conversation

Stories go away
Nobody knows where

We hear only our own voices
Still echoes returning to our emptiness

WORD HYPNOSIS

A word is dying, and thought is dying
Not in a word but by deceit
Not by substance but through hypnosis

A word becomes its own nemesis
Not a means of communication
But a means of waging war

JUST A FEW WORDS

Does he want to prove that he knows Greek and Latin,
Mythology and history of ancient people
Or did he want to write a poem?

When the long-bygone Lee Po wanted to say something
He could do it with only a few words.

THE SAME STORY

Where are all the people and their stories
All the noise and their quarrels

Hate gave birth to hate
Seeds scattered

We forget old stories
But those stories remain the same

THOUGHT

How alive is thought,
Invisible
Yet, without thought, there is no sight

How tough thought is
They try to break it
And it freely walks

How tall thought is
Smiling from far away
Observing us sadly

The depth of thought is its height—
The deeper thought is,
The taller it becomes.

A LIE

A lie is an illness
Or a condition for survival

Plague that easily spreads
Or a natural state of mind

Often more powerful than truth
A lie can suffocate us with sharp claws

Silently, we accept the bait
That pulls down even more

A smiling lie is a whirlwind
Easy to enter but hard to escape

Often more attractive than truth
It offers tomorrow instead of today

Truth is hard-hearted and unrelenting
A lie is much more imaginative

TRUTH AND LIE

Truth told the truth to the truth
The truth remained unsaid

Truth told the truth to the lie
A lie was told

A lie told a lie to a lie
A lie was told

Truth by truth annihilates itself
A lie by a lie multiplies

In the lie of truth lies the truth

SOCRATES

Socrates did not write
By conversing, he confessed

Teaching others
He corrected himself

He did not waste time
In a vain search for a place in history

Others made him a legend
Through which he talks even today

TIREDNESS

It has been a long voyage
Full of traps

We stand in wonder
Before a big Temple
Built long before us

After Homer and Dante,
Is a whole century of creating
Worth one Shakespeare

NEW WORD

How does one say something new
And not retell

Either all lights are turned off
Or inner light is missing

WHAT AFTER

DUMBNESS

He did not profess to anybody
How to reach others without professing

Others talked a lot
He carried his truth within himself

Saint or sage
Outcast or blessedly crazy

Neither did others need him
Nor did he need them

He died, and nobody noticed
So with him died his truth

ESTRANGEMENT

Suddenly you disappeared
We thought that you would always be here

We looked for you everywhere
And couldn't find you

Are you alive or dead
Will you message us?

Will you give us any sign
We fight; you toast your absence

Maybe you watch us from somewhere
Laughing at our inability

TAME SOUND

Look around
See if there is some other way

Scratch your memory
Go deep into yourself

If you follow the light
You will conquer both ways

This way or the other way
Are equally important

You not only are hunted by others
You unknowingly hunt yourself

HERE AND THERE

Do not look too far for
You will see nothing
Go far for a visit
But spend some time here as well
You will have lots to tell us
When you return
Unless you become mute
Along the way

CIRCUMSTANCES

Becoming closer to others
Through solitude
You don't give up

You do listen to their stories
About extraordinary events
All their fallacies

What really has to happen, you know, so
You move on with a smile
Stay in motion, irrespective of circumstances

Yet, you can decide
To stay in the same place
With the same enthusiasm

You are the main circumstance of your life
You don't wait for circumstances but create them
Building up yourself despite obstacles

It is not important how far you will go
But to enrich the lives of others and your own
With anything of value

A LANTERN

He went on distant trips
His home, he did not forget

He carried his home lantern inside himself
So when he went astray, he could find his way

A lot of time passed, and
He could hardly remember his home

The old man waited by the shore
For his own sunset

Once again, a lantern reminded him
At one time, he was indeed someone else

LIKE THIS AND LIKE THAT

Now that I am an old man
I see certain things
I could have done differently
But the story of every life
Ends in the same way
And would it really make a difference
This way or the other,
In the majestic story
Of the Universe that continues
Untouched, in its own way,
Anyway

WHAT AFTERWARD

You had to go through wonders
To be where you are
To tell your story
To give a chance to others

Everything seemingly looks easy
Yet, while you were traveling
Indeed, along the way,
There were temptations, and
You resisted.

You saw clear water and a tree
The bench on which you sit now
And looked through the water
To see what awaits you afterward.

KNIGHT

Devoted to your clear truth
You stand alone

Oppressed from all sides
You fly your own route

Either you will be you
Or you will not be at all

KNIGHTS

Ceremonials are dying
There are no real festivities

Nobody is surprised by anything
Faceless inhabitants occupy a sad world

In nurturing rituals
We nurture our characteristics,
Featured traits.

We are more comfortable today
But somehow, also sadly bored

Where are the people who did
Knightly deeds singing

We need new knights but
Without swords

GAMES

NO

Come out from within yourself
Speak out

You spent enough time sitting and waiting
Listened enough

Don't be an ant
Who moves in circles only

Say no!
Accept the burden of revenge

WAR

Coming into the world is the first war
The rest is a continuation
Acquiring strength for wars that await you

You will learn
Not to show feelings
Wearing various masks

You will not allow others
To see weeping that lasts
While pretending you are at peace
You will simulate

Wherever there is somebody else
A war is not far away.
Even if you are alone
You wage war with yourself.

THINGS

Silence the last flicker,
The final twinkle of resistance
Create paradise
By quenching the desire to look at sky
And look at things close by

A breeze, a forgotten summer, a smile
All can fit into a storefront window
Of happiness culled from advertisements
Smiling at our frightened faces

It was a long journey to get here
Robbed of our most intimate nature
In and around us,
We moved ever closer to a synthetic reality
We built tall buildings, but
We have not become any taller.

CHEAT

Don't surrender yet
You have already endured everything
Whatever others may say
They say it to deceive and comfort themselves
Not help you

CIRCUS

You listened for a long time
To those who like to talk

With time, you fell ill
Cleansing lasted for a long time

Today, you are afraid even of sincere stories
Something in your stomach always turns cold

Occasionally, anyway, you do return to the circus

HIS HIGHNESS

It was not possible to talk directly with His Highness;
Even if His Highness gave you that opportunity,
It was strenuous and insulting.
His Highness was not interested in others;
In his spare time, His Highness criticized and wrote memoirs.
His Highness thought nobody knew what he knew,
Because His Highness knew everything,
Known and unknown;
His Highness was always confident in his statements,
Especially about what he viewed for the first time;
Should you want a definite opinion,
Only ask His Highness;
His Highness never had any doubts about
The kind of Highness he is.
His Highness was angry
If you were not interested in his thoughts
Since our destiny depended on them.
One day, somebody remembered to open a valve;
His Highness flew high like a balloon;
He never returned.
It is sad without His Highness;
Now that we are all so smart
We don't easily find resolutions.

THE DWARF

He thought that others were small
That was his greatness

He thought others could also be bigger
But in other lives

He believed in reincarnation
He was at the top of previous lives

Tall and kind
He looked at the world from his height

Others grew
While he grew more stunted

This dwarf still observes the world
From his self-imposed height

VIRUS OF THE SOUL

If you could have walked on the planet
Before humans lived here
Maybe Ivory Coast would have seemed
More beautiful than *La Côte d'Azur*

We measure everything by ourselves
With almost a necessary conceit
Perhaps it's better that way

MERIT AND FAILURE

I did not produce anything of importance
You accuse yourself

But question yourself
If any good arises from it

Do not measure your place and value
By the flashy success of others

Do not compare anything in the external world
Your only real value is you

The measure of yourself
Is your own worth among your kin

Invisible traces are the light
That does not shine in an obvious way

This light shines in unpredictable ways
Over the lives you unselfishly affected

Good deeds are things of importance
The wealthiest people are those with the warmest hearts

The rest is not of colossal importance
Except for the cheap parade

LENGTHEN THE DAY

You want to extend the day
Maybe you will succeed further
Because day lives only in your head

Science is of no help with this challenging task

GAME I

Invent a new game when you are bored
Find the light within to inspire you

Even when Archimedes safeguarded his circles—
His was still a game,

With the same desire, Copernicus looked up at the heavens
Or Galileo Galilei after him

The game is when you look at treetops and clouds
Illuminating the world from within

If you wait for the light to appear,
Boredom will never leave you

GAME II

Even in dreams, we play games
In reflections, snow, and rainbows

There are no winners in real games
The game itself is bigger than the winning

A game is the only serious part

GAME III

Serious affairs and history
Are carefully laid snares for the uninformed

Creators of history always play
With our impotence and our ignorance

They entertain while you daydream
About seriousness and importance

You mark and celebrate errors
Transforming failures into successes

All those big words
Produce disgust today

Politicians are grocers
Ambitious clowns

They offer cookies and other sweets
They teach you to play their game

Say, thanks, and add—no
For a game, you don't need a teacher

Stars and idols
Arrogantly dance often

Who are those people?
Do you ever think to ask?

That is their game
Let them play it themselves

Refuse your support
Even without it, they will survive

But if you stay in their game
You will not survive

REFLECTION OF AN UPSET ONE

I growl
They irritated me
At the moment when I was born

They did not stop angering me until today
I cried at first
Today, I growl instead
I have huge eyeteeth

I don't know how I stood all that
They did not ask me
They decided for me

So here I am now
Waiting for the growling to pass
Then I will rest.

IS IT POSSIBLE TO WRITE A POEM

DOES GOD EXIST?

Should we doubt an eagle's flight
Or the Sun

Should we doubt a bee, a flower
Or so many humans?

This thought is more
A question of belief in our senses

It is not utterly illogical to believe
That we don't exist

Sight is still stronger than logic
Most of us believe in what we see

Faith is a question of eyesight
Even the blind can see that.

INSULT I

Holy books are an insult to a God
With good intentions

Who has the right to put words
In the mouth of an almighty Lord

Who has the right to spread a lie just
In the name of God

Still, God is merciful
Understands our need

Billions and billions of galaxies
Who knows how many civilizations there are

All have Holy books
Their own prophets and God's sons

GOD'S SON

The Universe is God's son
Who created many children
To fertilize the emptiness

He forgot what he was, so
He tries to remember
His problem is more the remembering
Than the problem of the truth

What he was and what he is—
Always one and the same;
He forgets himself
And longs to recall

CHRIST

For two thousand years already
They crucified an innocent Christ

What he was
Is different than what they wanted

Christ did not ask or want
To be what he was not

They do not need him
But want their own ideas about him

Pontius respected him
More than they

Burning the witch Giordano Bruno
Is one more wound inflicted on Christ's body

If he were to reappear
Those who hide behind him would
Only crucify him again

The idea is older than the Roman Empire
In all of it, Pilatus looked helplessly guilty

HEAD

Your head is a lit chamber
Thanks to it, you can stand darkness
Nourished by an inner light

This light opens the day
Extinguishes indifference
To tweets of water and ripples of birds
Such light multiplies space

The light teaches you to
Convert life into a festive promenade

LIFE

What we call life
Is only talk of nature.

Nothing is inanimate.
The rest is our interpretation.

A FLASH OF SILENCE

We like to admit to only that which already glows
Although it is nobler to support brightness
Before it glows, not afterward.
It is easy to see the glow
But it is hard to recognize
The awakening of silence.

By accepting this flash, this glow
We only join others
By understanding silence, we shine alone
Ourselves.

BENEFACTORS

Never be deceived by the goodness of air
Not all beings that breathe are good

Seductive singing is a trap
Disease often comes with a smiling face

Strangers are endearing
Because you don't know them yet

He who confided his deepest secret to you
Be always wary of his secret

Don't pay attention to those who offer too much

IS IT POSSIBLE TO WRITE A POEM

Is it possible to write a poem
Or are these words screams
Of outlaws exiled to the desert?

Is it possible to write a poem in the desert
Except for a poem about the sand
Which is a poem in and of itself

It's not easy to write a poem about a poem
Maybe doing so is even more difficult than writing a true poem
Although that is not redemption

BREAK

When a poem dies
That is not death
But rather the announcement
Of a new awakening.
The death of a poem is only a brief break,
A pause.

IMPASSE

Hope without love is hopeless.

PARALYSIS

You want to, but you can't;
It doesn't go, won't move.

You would like to soar
Yet you too often fall.

Everything is set against you
Yet you think this is not your fault.

FACE TO FACE

You don't know anything
But I know even less

Why are you trying to prove the opposite then
When I have admitted it to myself?

IF

If you are good
They say you are weak

If you know much
They say it's not wisdom

If you don't know
Then you are stupid

If you quote somebody else
You only quote

If you express your opinion
You act smart

If you contemplate
You live in the clouds

If you are slick
You cheat

You'll never be able to make them happy

THE OLD AND THE NEW PLACE

You think you are still in the old place
But you are already far from it

You believe in the old world
But the new one grows everywhere

You were absent from the old place
For a long time, carrying the old world with you

Yet never getting accustomed to the new place
You became a stranger both in it and in the old place

ABSURD

You wrote many poems
Yet you do not know if anybody will read them
Then Tertullian comes to mind
And you continue to write because it is absurd

INSULT II

You are afraid to escape the average
That would be hard for others somehow

Why would you think to insult them?
It is better to be united in equality

While you are equal
They will always find a way to prove you are inferior

Should you escape
You will help them to see themselves

But they would never forgive you that blessing.

HOAX

We see something is wrong
Helplessly, we accept others' helplessness
We stay silent

Nobody fights against weakness
That is why weakness has power
It becomes even more audacious

A THOUGHT ABOUT OURSELVES

If what we think of ourselves were true
The planet would overflow with geniuses

What we think about ourselves
Geniuses did not think of themselves

They blossomed
They did not talk about blossoming

They grew
They did not talk about growing

They knew they were not too great
We do not know that

Real geniuses would like that
What we think of ourselves is true

They would have a larger family
We would be less bored

Nevertheless, no genius can help us
Solve a problem so personal

A QUESTION FOR THE SUN

Pose your questions to the Sun
It will remain mute

Pose a question to a bird
You will get an honest answer if
You know the language of birds

Pose a question to the sea and listen
A question to the forest and stay silent

Pose your questions to people and
You will get countless useless answers

HAPPINESS SÉANCE

A magician, a wizard, asked the attendees
To join his séance in appreciation of happiness

He told beautiful stories
All the attendees listened in apt anticipation

Then, the magician engaged his apprentices
To talk instead of him

From anticipation, a wait matures
New magicians and new apprentices multiplied

The séance is still going on
It looks like it will never end

THE OLD BENCH

The bench on which he used to sit is empty
Nobody comes to this park anymore

To the former visitors, many a beautiful thought appeared
While they sat on this bench

After destructive fiends passed through
The park is abandoned

Evil is stronger than anybody imagined

GARDEN

From whichever side I start
I think I am in an old place
Where others have been before me

I take old roads
Hoping to find a new little path
For another new traveler

SOUND OF THE SILENCE

WHISPER YOUR SECRET TO ME

Whisper your secret to me
Share your solitude
Touch the other end of truth

Whisper your secret to me
You will not defeat solitude
For a moment, at least
Be a smile on someone else's face

EMPATHY

Come to my dream to dream
Your beauty and recognize it,
Come to sense and taste the light and breath,
All that reason is afraid to do.

If you give in to the power
Of the dazzle, the enchantment,
You'll find the sleeping secret,
In the well-imagined fairy tale
On the lip of my soul.

SOMEBODY ALWAYS WAITS

Nobility is not only in forgiveness.
Always remember Samaritans.
If you forget yourself, remember the others.

There is somebody whose worth depends on yours,
Whose senses crave your deeds;
Somebody of value always waits.

SIMPLICITY

You live and grow so naturally
That even a river will envy you

Comprehend, catch the silence
Where the captured treasure sleeps

Beyond all vanities, fights, and desires
Omnipotent silence lies

THE WAY

When you saw the Moon for the first time
You set out on the way,
Found the road.

Collecting questions and wonderments
You grew with each

There were no final answers
Either before or later

Slowly, you evolved away from the child within
Today, you don't ask anything

You don't wonder before anything
You don't wonder at all.

HELL AND PARADISE

Hell and paradise do exist
These are not empty stories
Illusion.

People burned by fiery tongs
Hopeless orphans scattered round

Formidable claws catch all fugitives
Devour more pitiable bodies

But then, to some, Hell is nice and warm
On the scary fields of paradise

The sky and sea generously merge
For the lucky inhabitants of such a paradise

FLAVOR OF THE FIELD

Where are all the games
Whispering, chirping, barking, the noise,
Fuming over roofs in wintertime?
Where is that old fairy tale?

The fields had flavor;
We ran and sought out something.
Who are you, who am I, who are they?
These questions came later.

CURE

What goes on
In the Amazons of our souls,
In the galaxies of our nerves,
Our instincts, senses?

Hellenes had no psychotherapy;
They didn't need it.

New creations, products of our brains, arrived
Yet, the number of mentally disturbed still grew.

A LIGHT BEAM

Invisible rays do fall on you
A ray from far merges with your inner ray

The game can continue
As long as one ray can find another

THE DAY

You are parting with this day
Waiting for another
Thankful to the sky

As long as the day watches from you
You are on a safe path

BEETHOVEN AND DEATH

EXITS

He stepped on the threshold of wonders
To try and find the exit

He wanted to fly, so
The road widened before him

A courageous player he was, so
He flew from one space to another

A storm was his Nirvana
When everything became silent

He understood no place was left
For his return.

SECRET

Rich and distant
You silently wait

Where do you hide?
Offer a pointed sign
Invite us as your guests

Encircled by the sea
Negligent or only too self-sufficient
You don't want to open the door

SECRET AND THE TRUTH

There are many secrets
Don't try to resolve them all

There are many truths
Only look to one aim

All truths come from one

TREASURY OF THE SOURCE

Don't miss out, fail to see
How flowers and the seagulls
Are cheered by the Sun
Accept them

Look out through the darkness
Dream through light,
Fly toward the core, the central point
From which you set out
On your voyage.

BEETHOVEN AND DEATH

Death is at the door,
Said Beethoven.
Should we believe him?
Maybe he did not mean to joke,
Maybe he really saw death,
Maybe their eyes met.
There was nobody there to tell him
To lock the door instead.

SAME SIGHT

When emptiness sees,
It always sees the same.

If we were to understand
How important it is to say something
And say it well,
Maybe we wouldn't write a single word
But that would be tragic.

MAYBE

To leave without a greeting, a salute, or a goodbye
There is no need to bother anyone

Silently set out and
Nobody will notice any movement

No person will ever recognize
The absence of what has never been seen

What is not seen does not exist
And what is seen is an illusion

There is a thought that cannot be told
There is a meaning that does not need approval

Silence is rewarding and hospitable
Just like life can be on a brighter side

Judgmental and dangerously beautiful
Life rewards and punishes with equal force

Every human being leaves valuable traces
Untraceable.

EPILOGUE

INFERNO

There are countless circles of hell;
Believers never penetrate the Ninth Circle.

In the squeeze of a storm,
The guards rushed out of the dark entrance hall.
Under web-covered eyes, there are devices
With invisible antennas connected to its headquarters.

Butterflies cover the horizon
With the red-black drapery of their wings.

Howling voices in solo
And the clanging of the darkness
Relate the truth of this place.

There, where the echoes
Of butterfly's wings can be heard,
The doors to Inferno opened.

ABOUT THE AUTHOR

Dejan Stojanović was born in Peć in 1959. He graduated from the Law School of the University of Priština. He has published books of poems:

The Sun Observes Itself (Sunce sebe gleda), NIP Književna reč, Belgrade, 1999.

The Sign and Its Children (Znak i njegova deca), Prosveta, Belgrade, 2000.

The Creator (Tvoritelj), Narodna knjiga, Belgrade, 2000.

The Shape (Oblik), Gramatik, Podgorica, 2000.

The Dance of Time (Ples vremena), Konras, Belgrade, 2007.

Pentalogy: *The World in Nowherness (Svet u nigdini)*:

1. Ozar (Ozar), Udruženje književnika Srbije, Belgrade, 2017.

2. The World and God (Svet i Bog), Udruženje književnika Srbije, Belgrade, 2017.

3. The World in Nowhereness (Svet u nigdini), Udruženje književnika Srbije, 2017.

4. The World and Humans (Svet i ljudi), Udruženje književnika Srbije, Belgrade, 2017.

5. The Home of Light (Dom svetlosti). Udruženje književnika Srbije, Belgrade, 2017.

The Hidden Light (Skrivena svetlost), Čigoja, Belgrade, 2018.

Primordial Spark (Iskra iskona), Albatros plus, Belgrade, 2021.

Centuries and Steps (Vekovi i koraci), Albatros plus, Belgrade, 2023.

Essays:

Creator and Creating (Stvaralac i stvaranje), Albatros plus, Belgrade, 2021.

The New Man and the New World (Novočovek i novosvet), Rad, Belgrade, 2022.

Anthology: *Selected Serbian Plays* (*Izabrane srpske drame*), USA, 2016.

Philosophy: *Absolute*, New Avenue Books, USA, 2024.

A book of his selected interviews, Conversations, was published in 1999 by NIP Književna reč, Belgrade. The Serbian Heritage Foundation and the Association of Writers of Serbia for Intellectual Engagement awarded the book the Rastko Petrović Prize.